AUGERINO AMORE

A MATCHED BY THE UNICORN STORY

BRITTANY LAWRENCE

Edited by: Writers Wingman llc

Cover by: Unfortunate Design

This is 100% created by humans. Generative AI was not used in any part of the writing, editing, or production of this book. We support human artists, first and always.

Published in the United States by Writers Wingman llc.

AUGERINO AMORE

Joanna Moonbeam is a circus kid turned farrier who has always let the wind take her where it may. Now it's blown her into a small mountain town of Middle Park, Colorado, where she might just see herself falling in love or into one of the giant sinkholes plaguing the town. Fine time to join a magical dating app run by a unicorn. It would take real magic to find her someone to date way out there.

AUTHOR'S NOTE

This paranormal romance leans to cozy but has some high-stakes suspense. Please review the following before reading:

This story contains Sexual innuendos, nudity, talk of : roofies, dating safety precautions, abusive ex-boyfriends, loss, and depression.

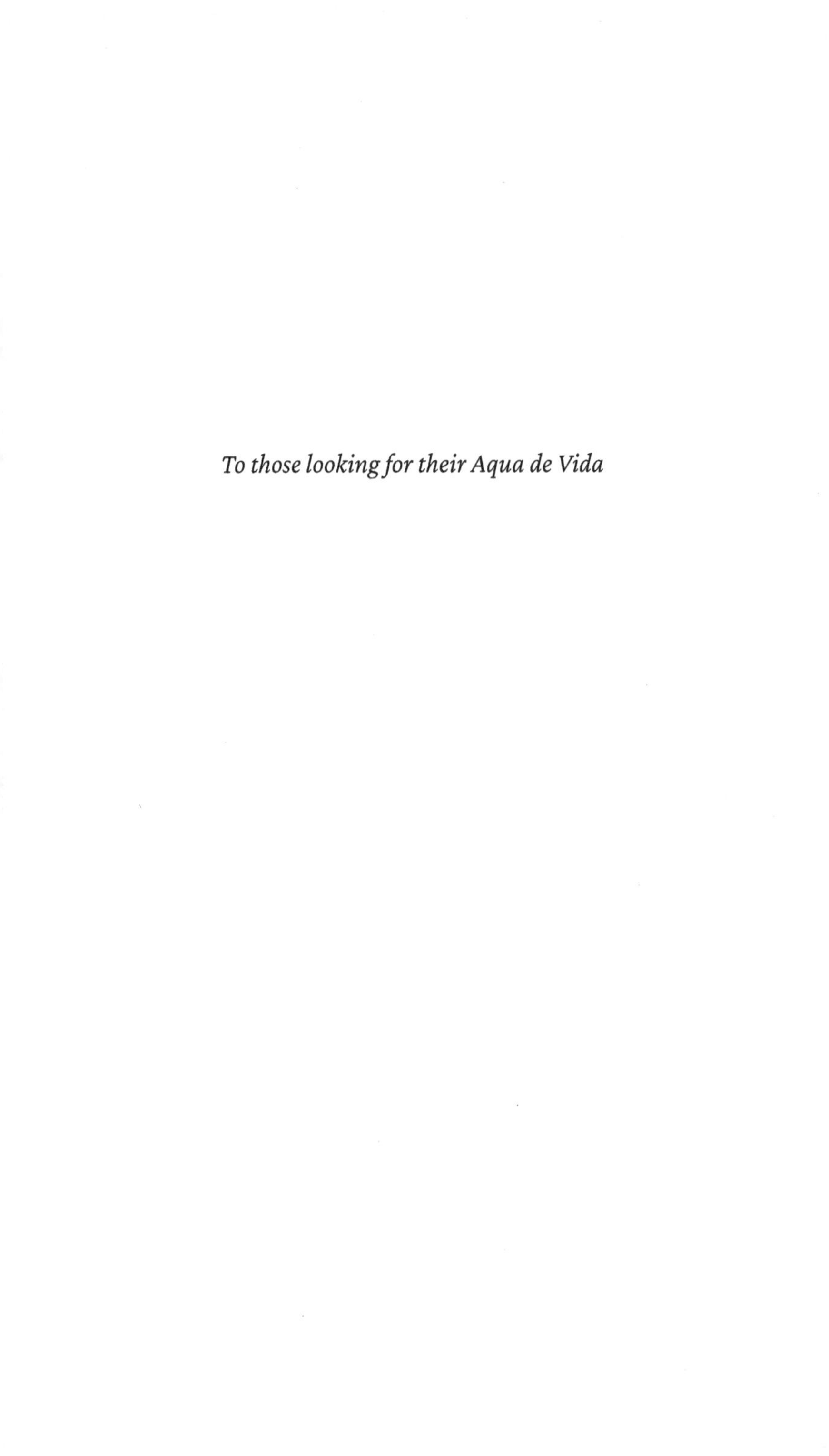

To those looking for their Aqua de Vida

CHAPTER ONE

Middle Park Colorado was out there. But I didn't realize how far in the boonies it was. Working as a traveling farrier, I had the option of going where the wind blew, but I was beginning to think this was a little too middle of nowhere, even for me. The closest campground was over an hour away, and the "town" was so small it didn't have stop signs at the only intersection. There was a small grocer, a tool shop, and a game and feed store.

That was it.

I'd been to different small towns doing this job, but this one took the prize of smallest.

The add for the job included medical, dental, with room and board on property.

While I loved my van, she needed some work. The shower and toilet were nice, but I avoided using them as much as I could. No one liked cleaning out the gray and black lines. Especially me. When I could, I would visit my subscription gym for showers and take bathroom breaks at gas stations to avoid it.

When I pulled up to the empty field, I didn't worry about getting a ticket. That meant there had to be police nearby. With no police station in town, the likelihood was slim. Did I need to worry about a disgruntled property owner knocking on my door? Sure. But I'd hear them way before I would see them, and Shrimp would hear them before I would. I wasn't really worried. And I didn't start work until tomorrow, so I didn't want to show up at the ranch before I had to. I'm a committed employee, but not that committed.

I put the car in park and checked in on Shrimp. The blue heeler was lying on my bed, happy as a pig in shit. Which was far from how I was feeling after that long drive through some sus mountain roads that hadn't been plowed yet. There wasn't much snow on the ground, but it was early January in Colorado. There were plenty of dark spots around mountain curves that turned the roads into ice.

Normally, I would have opened the back door to let some fresh air in and Shrimp run out to take a wee, but he wasn't moving, and I wasn't going to make him. I was ready to lay down next to him and let my arms rest for a little while. I'd parked about 20 minutes out from the ranch. So, we were in a good place to stop for the night.

I pulled my phone from my pocket and checked for service. Surprisingly, I had internet. Must have been because I was close enough to the ranch? Either way, I was grateful.

Haley had texted me, asking if I'd tried out the dating app she'd sent me. I'd downloaded it, but never opened it. But I'd promised I'd give it a go. So, I opened the unicorn app. The unicorn with the rainbow afro danced around my screen, glitter cascading off it.

“Are you looking for love? Are you willing to let magic

take the reins? If so, you must be open to meeting and interacting with your match for one date. Details will be sent to you about your prearranged date once you've been matched.

"Should you find you're not a match, you're wrong, but you can walk away.

"By accepting these terms, you will not hold Miriam's Date-a-Base liable for true love's kiss or any magical experiences thereafter. We may use any photos submitted to us as marketing materials for those looking for love."

Pretty sure this wasn't the app for me. I was more of a kiss right now kind of gal, never mind true love. But I clicked on the little box to accept, anyway. The other dating apps I'd tried hadn't been all that helpful with a 'fun for now' relationship either. So I entered my basic information and hit next.

The little screen exploded in glitter. "Jo, you found a match!"

Where was the questionnaire? The personality quiz? Was it really spyware, and were they looking into my phone's use and stealing all of my information? There was no way I matched with someone out here in the middle of nowhere. They must have picked up on the city when I downloaded the app.

"Wear dancing boots, and put on your thinking caps. Be prepared to show off all of your moves on your date, should you chose to continue."

At this point, I was vaguely interested. And mildly panicked I had just leaked all of my information and would have to deal with a stolen identity. But the graphics were really cute, and it didn't *feel* bad. And if I knew anything, it was that my intuition spoke in statements and anxiety spoke in questions.

"What the hell, why not?"

I tapped the little unicorn. It flew around the screen again. "Your date will meet you tonight at 7pm, 1087 Tuft Road."

The address on my map app said it was a small bar known for its flaming hot wings. There wasn't much else posted online, but it was only about thirty minutes from the main road. I had three hours before I had to be there. Long enough for a nap with Shrimp, and a refresh before dinner.

I set my alarm and settled into bed. Shrimp rested his head on my shoulder, his cold nose a breath away from my ear. Silly Shrimp.

CHAPTER TWO

A cold nose and a warm lick to the face woke me up. I looked down at my phone; I still had seven minutes left on my timer before I had to get up and get ready to go.

Shrimp let out an exaggerated sigh as he stretched and hopped down onto the floor. I had to get up now because this guy really needed to get out there and use the restroom, and probably get some zoomies out.

The door opened, and the cold crept in. It slowed Shrimp down a little bit, but once he warmed up his joints, he was as spry as a young pup.

I threw on my favorite oversized sweater over my tank, applied some lip gloss, fluffed my sandy blonde hair, and called it good. We were meeting at a bar, there wasn't a reason to dress up. But I would find my nice boots. No way was I going to be dancing in flip-flops.

Shrimp chased after something going a mile a minute and disappeared from view. "Shrimp!"

He whimpered, the sound grew distant as if he had gone over a cliff. I flung the door closed behind me and ran in the same direction, being mindful of where I was going. We were in the valley of a mountain range. I didn't think there was some random drop offs but who was I to know these parts?

"Shrimp!" I shouted breathlessly as I caught up to him.

He was stranded in a hole easily three feet wide. Had I kept driving into the valley, I'd have wrecked the van and probably gotten hurt.

Shrimp's tail wagged hard enough his whole body was wiggling with him.

"You doing okay, bud?" I asked.

He gave a quick, happy bark. He wasn't limping, and it didn't look like he had hurt himself. The hole was deep. Even at nine years old, Shrimp could nearly jump over my parents' eight-foot privacy fence. So it had to be deeper than that.

What did I have in the van I could slide down in there for him to climb out of? Because if I were to go in there, we'd both be stuck.

Did I have rope and a way to pull him up?

Racing back to the van, I lifted the door on the floor that help my work supplies. I had a twelve-foot lead rope, and a pair of leather chaps I wore for work. I knotted up the ends to create a basket for Shrimp to step into and tied it up as best I could with the rope.

Slinging the rope and the chap-basket over my shoulder, I walked back to Shrimp. He was sitting at the bottom of the pit like the good, patient boy he was.

I lowered the chaps down into the pit next to him. Shrimp weaved in and out of the rope, tail wagging, looking up at me. "Good boy!" I said, waiting for him to get into the middle of the chaps. He danced around a little bit, then slowed down. "Good Shrimp! Sit!" Shrimp planted his butt as close to the middle of the chaps as I was gonna get. "Okay, Shrimp, I'm gonna raise you up now. Stay still. Stay!"

Planting my feet securely, well enough away from the edge of the hole, I leaned back and pulled. When I realized I was not making quick work of this with my arms, I leaned back even more and walked away from the hole. I really needed to work on my upper body at the gym.

Shrimp was the bestest boy, until the ledge and who could blame him getting squished by the edge of the hole and the trap I'd built for him. He yelped as I pulled him over the edge, then floundered around the rope as he hurried over to me.

His wet nose met my cheek, followed by kisses. "I love you to Shrimpy. Let's walk back to the car and stay by momma."

I wound up the rope and dangled the chaps over my shoulder. I'd unknot them when I got back to the car and put them away immediately.

Why were there random holes in the middle of the valley? Were there more holes? What were people looking for out here?

I knew there were old cowboy tales of treasure; miners and bandits had hidden away, but it was all lore. Nothing ever came of it.

With everything stored and locked up, I had just enough time to get to the bar and only be fashionably late.

CHAPTER THREE

The bar was a standard Western bar with neon signs and a gravel parking lot.

I parked under a tall tree, though I couldn't have told you what kind it was. Then turned back to Shrimp, situated on the bed. I filled his water bowl, pulled out his favorite chew toy from the cabinet over the sink, and turned on the heated blanket waiting on the bed for him. Ruffling his ears, I kissed his head until he rolled away from me like an indignant teenager.

"I know, I know. I love you, Shrimp. I'll be back in a little bit."

I locked the car and stuffed my keys in my jeans pocket with my phone and tiny wallet.

There weren't many cars in the parking lot, so the crowd of people was impressive. Either they were all about carpooling with a designated driver, or they lived close enough to walk in the snow to their favorite bar. It was hopping in here. Each table of trivia players, no doubt.

I went to the bar, where there was open seating, and

pulled out my phone while I waited for the bartender to make their way to me.

The unicorn flew across my screen. "Your date will be in all red! Keep your eyes open." Surveying the bar, there was plenty of blue and black, even a little orange sprinkled in but no red. They must have been behind as well. I wish the app would tell me their name, or at least what gender I was looking for. I wasn't picky about who warmed my bed, so long as I got to share it with someone.

"What can I get ya?" the young bartender asked. She barely looked legally old enough to serve me, nonetheless drink herself.

I pointed to the man sitting next to me and the bottle of beer he was holding. "I'll take one of those." I wasn't a snooty beer person, but I did prefer a bottle.

She grabbed one from behind the bar, and I watched as she opened it. I slid my card over, "Can you start a tab?"

"Yeah. You here for trivia? They've got another five minutes of collecting names down by the DJ." She pointed at the end of the bar where a man stood with a microphone.

"I am, thanks. Can I also get a menu?"

She nodded and slid over a bar menu with two small pieces of paper and a pencil. I took one more look around the bar to see if anyone in red had shown up. My phone didn't show any notifications, and the unicorn didn't dance across my screen.

So, I named our team The Small Town Circus. I'd explain when they got here. As I made my way to the end of the bar to submit my team name, I took one last glance around. Nada. I took a swig of my beer and found my earlier seat waiting for me.

The bartender returned, "Can I get anything started in the kitchen for ya?"

"Yeah, I'll take a basket of boneless wings and fries."

She held out her hand for the menu and put my order in.

I looked down at my phone one last time as the Trivia Master started their schpeal about cheating on phones and the rules of the game. The unicorn danced across my phone, "You're date is running late, keep faith he will make it."

He. He was enough to know he was going to be late. Did I have faith in men? No. Not really. Did I think they were beautiful creatures and a lot of fun? Sure. But when it came to taking care of business, or following through with commitments, I didn't hold my breath.

Trivia was fun, even solo. The wings were almost as good as the reviews said they would be. But the fries! I'm not sure what spices they put on them, but they had a touch of heat and sweet. It was worth being stood up for.

While I didn't win Trivia, the team of old ladies in matching sweaters were so cute to watch their responses to each question, win or lose.

As I settled up the tab with the bartender, I asked, "Do you mind if I sleep in the parking lot for the night? I'm knew to the area and I'm not sure if I can get back to my campsite in the dark."

Her eyes grew wide, and her mouth stretched to the edges of her face in a frown. "Eeek, I'm not sure. Let me get the boss lady."

The woman the bartender came back with, looked like a goddess. Tall, broad, sleek dark hair cascaded over her shoulders. "I hear you need a place to sleep." She eyed me up and down.

"Yes, I have a van out front for my dog Shrimp and I. I just don't want to get lost on my way back to the campsite."

"You're not running anything out of your van are you?" She asked, her warm tone gone icy like a switch.

"No, ma'am. I'm a farrier. Starting work at the Las Casas Ranch tomorrow." I said.

Her shoulders fell, and her smile was back. "Oh, you must be Joanne! Bart told me about you the other day. Just in time for stock show season. Well, welcome. You can park in the lot for the night. Bart'll get you set up tomorrow at the ranch."

I finished off my beer. "Do you work with Mr. Las Casas?"

"Bart? In a sense. He takes care of my patrons and I take care of them. Most in here work for him in one way or another. Bart's a good boss to work for. Hardest working man I ever met. He'll take good care of you." She tapped the bar, "Excuse me." She said and helped a man waving her down.

I took my beer bottle and put it in the trash can on the way out.

The cool winter air was a slap in the face. I'd gone from cozy and mellow to awake just like that. While it seemed like a nice small town, I made sure no one was sitting out for a smoke or following me around to my car. Quickly getting into my van, I locked and added my security bar to the side door. Then I used the seat belts from the two front seats to wrap around the car handle before I buckled them back up. I wasn't paranoid, but I was cautious.

Putting up my foam insulation to black out the windows, I tried to keep the noise to a minimum, being Shrimp was already snoring.

He didn't stir from his heated dog bed. It was on a timer so it wouldn't overheat. In about thirty minutes, he'd be crawling into bed with me.

I slipped off my boots, slid some toothpaste onto my toothbrush and scrubbed away as I stripped down to a t-shirt and panties. I wasn't one for a long, drawn-out evening ritual, or morning for that matter. Clean teeth, clean clothes, call it good.

Then I slipped into bed, set my alarm, and drifted off to sleep with the sounds of the winter breeze blowing in a storm strong enough to shake the car.

CHAPTER
FOUR

Shrimp indeed joined me in bed. Which was great because it did get cold. We'd insulated my van so much you'd think it would keep the heat in and the cold out, but boy, the winters could test a girl.

When my alarm went off, Shrimp didn't move and protested when I did. But I needed to be on time and ready to work when I got to the Las Casas Ranch.

I dressed in layers. Tank, flannel, jacket. Long Johns , jeans, and a thick pair of wool socks. I was cozy, and I'd need to be if I was going to bee outside or in a cold stable working.

A hot cup of coffee and a cold bowl of cereal later, we were on our way. Shrimp was pouting, having no interest in going potty this early in the morning.

The drive to the ranch was a short one. Less than thirty minutes from the bar to the ranch. I wonder which had been built first, and how much time they'd put into purchasing the property.

Pretty brilliant.

The Ranch's entrance from the road had a huge arch

made of thick ringed pieces of wood and a sign with the emblem reading de Las Casas Ranch.

The property was stunning. Rolling fields of golden majesty, and a tree lined road lead to the main house. It was two stories, and you could tell it was as old as the settlers in this area. But it was maintained with such admiration and care it looked damn near new.

I parked on the side of the gravel driveway. There wasn't much snow left over here, and what was,, was sure to be gone by noon.

From the front door of the ranch, a short, broad man with thick dark hair approached me, his hand outstretched. "Olah, welcome." He said eyes wide in surprise. "You must be Joanna."

"Call me Jo." I said.

"Jo." He said, his eyes warming and his smile softening. His hands were rough but strong. He had been in this business a long time.

"I'm Bartolomé de las Casas. Thank you for making it here so quickly. John from the R and R ranch spoke highly of you. My normal farrier's wife is expecting any day now, a little early, and it's our policy to give employees generous leave."

"Generous leave, what are you talking about?"

Farriers were paid at the point of service, much like a human nail tech. We didn't have salaried jobs.

"At Las Casas I employ all my care team full time. I include company housing because we are, well, out here. But you don't have to work every day unless there i's an animal in destress. The pay is less than what you'll find traveling but the perks out way the downsides."

That's why the listing said twenty thousand. I thought I'd spend a weekend here, pocket twenty k and move on.

But maybe it would be worth settling down some roots. If f nothing else, it would be nice to be somewhere with a bathroom I didn't have to clean out completely..

"I can't guarantee two years, but I'd like to see where this goes. If I decide the road is calling my name, I'll give you plenty of notice."

Bart held out his hand. "That''s a deal." He held out his hand toward the barn. "Follow me."

"I do have one more caveat."

He put his hands in his jeans pockets. "Shoot."

"I have a dog."

Bart's eyes narrowed, and he took a deep breath. "What kind of dog?"

I TOOK a few steps back and opened my van door to reveal ShrimpShrimp sitting at attention like the goodest boy he was.

"Ah, blue heeler. Working dog." Bart waved him over. "He's welcome to any part of the property, just be mindful of him. There's some big holes popping up out there on the east pasture, try to keep him from there. Don't know how long he might get stuck down there. I've fenced off the area but these things just keep popping up."

He put his hands on his hips and shook his head.

"I am familiar with them." I said.

"What?"

"Shrimp got stuck in one last night about thirty minutes east of the bar."

"I didn't realize they were popping up outside of our property." Bart crossed his arms and looked out to the east. "Anyway, follow me and I'll take you to the barn, where you can make yourself at home. I had Mark, my other farrier, pack up his things and leave the space for you to make yourself comfortable."

Comfortable? That wasn't something in a farrier's vocabulary. We carried our tools, worked long, hard, back breaking hours, but rarely did we ever have a space that we could get comfortable or settled, in.

"What kind of animals will I be working with?"

Bart opened the tall red doors to the barn. "Clydesdales, mostly." He held the door long enough for both me and Shrimp to get through. "But we also have a whole field of cattle and a mess of sheep. Four goats. And a resident coyote family. Though, the latter won't be a bother to either of us. Might see them around, though.

The barn was nice. Nothing special, , but wit was kept up. YoYou could tell they cared about their farm.

How I had never heard of this place before today was a mystery. Maybe because they were so far out here and employed in house?

The horses were magnificent! Tall, broad babies ranging in color from sable to gray.

They'd made an entire stall a little workshop, and honestly, this made so much sense. I couldn't wait to move all of my things in.

"Think you can make this work?" Bart asked.

"You'd be amazed by what I can make work." I said. Most of the time it was given a shady spot and a stool. Sometimes the farm would have a livestock crush, and those were great, but it was usually outside, and those days got hot quick.

CHAPTER FIVE

Shrimp and I set back and forth from the van to the barn. It didn't take long to get all of my supplies set out and organized. I packed light.

Bart moved hay from the top of the barn down into the stalls he'd previously cleaned. I watched him clean another three stalls before I went to interrupt him.

His flannel had been discarded and the long sleeve shirt he wore underneath was rolled up at the sleeves. The button at the neck popped open to reveal a tuft of short, black, curly chest hair. Sweat beaded on his forehead, and I wondered where the stable hands were, or if he did this every day, all day.

"I'm all set up." I said, catching his attention.

He wiped his brow with his forearm. "Good to hear." He said, then went back to spreading hay around the stall.

"Do you want me to start on any specific animals?"

HE LOOKED BACK over his shoulder at me, then leaned on the rack he was using. It was taller than he was, standing up right. "Nah, walk around. Get acquainted with the farm. Mi Casa e su casa. I'll show you your lodging when I'm done here."

"You sure? I can give you a hand."

Bart ran a hand through his hair, and boy, did that do something for me. "You're a farrier, right?"

"Yes." I wasn't sure I liked where this was going.

"Is helping me part of your job description?"

I crossed my arms. "No, it's not."

Bartolomé skewered the rake into the loose hay and stepped toward me. He spread his arms wide, leaning toward me as he held each side of the open stall.

Looking up at me, he said. "We each have our rolls here. If I need you're help I'll ask for it. But if I am a poor enough man to mismanage my help, I deserve to fail."

He held his arm out toward the barn door. "Go, explore. I'll find you soon."

I didn't know what to say, so I said nothing, calling Shrimp we I left the barn. In search of, I wasn't sure.

My phone dinged, and I received another text message.

"Jo! Your match would like to try again. What do you say?"

Two floating cloud buttons hovered on the screen. Yes and no.

I hit yes. Why not? What did I have to lose? And if it turned out poorly, well, everyone here would probably know because it was a small town and everyone knew everything in a small town.

The grounds were beautiful. The rolling hills were covered in grasses and wild flowers. Evergreens and aspens littered around like sprinkles on cupcakes. I'd always loved the mountains. Never spent a whole lot of time in them, as my job kept me on the prairie more than the mountains.

Before that, my parents would move us around with the circus. And with all the moving, I still kept coming back here. To the purple mountains and the golden waving plains. Colorado was home.

CHAPTER SIX

It was maybe another hour before Bart knocked on my van's door while Shrimp and I had lunch.

I opened the door; he'd found his flannel and thrown it on, which made me sad I wouldn't get to see those sculpted forearms again. But it was probably for the best I didn't lust after my boss. Workplace relationships always turned out messy. At least for me, they did.

"I'm just finishing up lunch." I said and waved him into the van. "Care to join us? I have more fix'ins for sandwiches."

He smiled and shook his head. "You're too nice, you know that?"

I'd never been told I was too nice before. Been called a lot of things, but too nice wasn't one of them.

"You want a sandwich or not?"

He shook his head and stepped into the van. "This is a nice set up. When you're done with your meal, we can drive it over to your new home while you're here."

I packed up the fixing for the sandwich, threw my plate in the sink, wrapped my sandwich up in a paper towel and sat in the driver's seat. I pointed to the passenger seat, then buckled myself in.

"We can go now." I said.

Bart sat down, buckled his belt, and pointed toward the dusty road that led between the barn and the main house. "Follow that road."

"Am I parking behind back?" I asked.

"Naw, only family stays in the main house."

"Oh." I said, stuffing a bite of sandwich in my mouth before I said something stupid. Like I thought your employees were like family or some other corny bullshit employers tried to sell so they worked harder and longer hours. Though it didn't sound like Bart was that kind of guy.

The road wound around the barn, back between the tree line and the large pasture on the other side of the barn.

There were six tiny homes about a hundred feet from one another. They looked like carbon copies of each other, but in different colors with crisp white trim. Different trees and parcels where gardens would grow in the summer were decorated with Christmas lights still.

The tiny house, painted blue with white trim, was devoid of any decorations, but was clean and orderly.

Bart pointed to the gravel driveway next to the house. There was no awning to park under, so I'd be cleaning the van off when it snowed, and cooling it off before I got in when it was warm. But it still looked cute as a button.

I parked the car, and we got out. I whistled for Shrimp and they raced out of the driver's seat and set to sniffing around.

Bart pulled out a keychain with two keys on it. He unlocked the door, opened it, and held the keys out to me. "You're welcome to decorate how you like. We try to keep a curfew of ten pm but you'll find everyone quiets down sooner than that for work. And because there's something magic about these mountains."

"Who are my neighbors?" I asked.

He waved me after him back outside. Next to me was a little red house. "Your immediate neighbor is Harper. She's the resident mechanic. Works on all our farming equipment and vehicles. If your van needs any work, she'd be happy to help.

"Next door to her," he said, pointing to the yellow house. "Is Joeseph. He's our animal ambassador. You'll get to know each other real well. He knows every animal here. He's not a veterinarian, but in two years he will be."

Bart pointed over to the purple house next. "That's Maria's house. She lives with her two kids, Mark and Matthew. She manages all the money here. If there's ever a discrepancy with your pay, you'll talk to her."

"I wouldn't talk to you?"

Bart crossed his arms and shook his head. "This land is older than I am. Been in my family for generations. I was raised around the horses. Not the books. My uncle never intended to for this ranch to fall into my hands. But here we are."

"How did you end up with the job?" I asked, knowing I was probably toeing the line of polite conversation.

Bart took a deep sniff and looked off at the farm. "Uncle left it to me." He cleared his throat. "Which leads me to my only request, no liquor on the farm. You're welcome to drink at the bar in town, but I don't like it on my farm. If you're hung over, don't come in to work. Just sleep it off and we can pick up where we need to."

"Do people drink a lot out here?" I wasn't a big drinker,

but I wanted to know if my close neighbors would come knocking on my door in a stupor.

"No. But we all enjoy a drink in town every once in a while. I just don't like it on the farm." His smile sagged a little. His shoulders fell forward.

"Who lives in the last two houses?" I pointed to the green and orange house at the end of the line of houses.

His eyebrows perked up along with his smile. "Sam and Wendy lived in the orange house until last month. He's my resident farrier. And it'll stay empty for him until we know if he's coming back. But for now, they've moved in with Wendy's parents who live in Denver. Closer to medical staff and family to help with the baby. It's hard to be a kid out here."

Maria's boys must be going through it.

"The green house is Page's. She's my property manager. Oversee's anything else on the property that needs done. Ever have a problem with your house, she's the one to talk to.

"Enjoy settling in." Bart held out the keys again, and this time I took them. He looked down at his watch, hopped down the stairs, and started off the way we came.

"You want a ride back to the house?" I hollered after him.

He put his hands in his pockets. "Naw, I'm heading to the glamp ground."

"You have a glamp ground?"

He spread his arms wide. "You see all this land? Gotta maximize on the property, or why have it?"

I laughed as I gave him a wave, and he turned around, trotting off to wherever the glamp ground was.

CHAPTER
SEVEN

I spent the rest of the day settling into the tiny house. There was a full mini kitchen which was huge compared to my small travel setup in the van. Even a stackable washer and dryer next to the fridge.

The lofted bedroom over the kitchen had an amazing view of the valley. And I couldn't wait to watch the snow fall from up here.

In all, it took me maybe four hours to unpack my things and start a load of laundry. It was going to be so nice not to have to find a laundromat.

Then I eyed the shower and knew I had to try it out.

It was easily four times as big as my little setup on the van and the only feet who had been on it were mine and whoever lived here before. The place was cleaned from top to bottom. I couldn't find a speck of dust if I tried. If only I could keep it this clean. Between me and Shrimp, that was nearly impossible.

The water hissed in the shower until it went up an octave, and I knew it was warm enough to get in. Steam escaped the minute I opened the glass door. The hot water melted my tight muscles, and I never wanted to leave.

I reached out for my shampoo, and I had to take a step to get it. I'd have to get used to that. There was enough room in here to easily fit another person or two. And boy, did that sound like a dream. Sharing this space with another person. Strong arms wrapping around me after a long, hard day's work. The soap suds-ing as we washed away the day's sweat.

It was too bad that the date had fallen through last night.

I turned off the hot water and, with it, let that bit of disappointment flow down the drain. I was here for work, not for pleasure. A whole year of no pleasure. Because small towns are small. And this one was probably the smallest I had ever been to.

And that's saying a lot, having worked on most of the ranches around Colorado.

I turned the water off, knowing I needed to invest in a bucket to collect the runoff while I waited for it to get warm. We were in a drought, and I had to do my part. Or at least feel like I was doing something.

The water would turn cool quickly, and I didn't stick around to see how cold the well water could get.

As I toweled off, my phone dinged. But not its normal ding. A quick repetition of four dings I'd never heard before.

Wrapped in my towel, I padded over to the sink where I'd set my phone. On the screen, the little unicorn from yesterday danced around. I tapped at the glitter and, "You're match wants to try again. Are you open to giving them s'more chances?"

I rolled my eyes at the pun. I tapped yes because, really, what else was I going to do?

"You'll meet at Le Casa Glamping, for bbq, s'mores, and a little stargazing, if the weather cooperates."

Where were Le Casa's glamp grounds?And what on earth was a glamp ground? A fancy campground? Something for celebrities? What could be glamorous about camping? There's dirt, and bugs, and a campfire. But I didn't see the glamour. Sure, it's still fun, but glamorous was not the adjective I'd have picked.

The screen popped up a map with a pin in it and an estimated walking time of fifteen minutes, or a five minute drive. Which was more my speed. I wasn't interested in waking in the dark to who knew where when there were bears and mountain lions lurking in the cold.

My limited wardrobe was already unpacked in my new closet. I took a breath and just sighed it out toward the organized closet. It wouldn't stay this way, but it was so nice while it lasted.

The question was, what was I going to wear?

CHAPTER EIGHT

I'd gone with a simple pair of jeans, boots—the cute kind, not the utilitarian kind—with a matching jean jacket over a thick, chunky, red-brown sweater.

This had been the warmest winter I'd ever experienced. Frankly, most of the state had ever experienced. The snow hadn't fallen, and it was unseasonably warm. Nearly what we would have expected in spring. Yet, it was still the peak of winter. If we didn't get some serious water and snow soon, we'd have a crazy fire season this summer and fall.

Shrimp was settling in right at home now, too. He'd found a new pee spot outside and rushed back in. Like he knew there were things older than any of us lurking in the trees. And I didn't blame him. I wasn't so sure about meeting someone I didn't know in the middle of the woods either. Surely a dating app wouldn't set me up on a murderous date, right? This wasn't a classifieds forum.

As I tugged on the doorknob to make sure it was locked, I glanced over at my nearest neighbor. Harper, was it? Maybe I should tell her where I was going in case something happened, and then they could send a search party.

I walked around her manicured rock garden, up the three steps to her door, and gave it a quick knock.

She shouted a "hold on!" the other side of the door, and I didn't wait long before she opened it. Her long brown hair spilled nearly to her waist in a tight braid. Her sharp features matched her demeanor. "Hey." She said.

"Hey, um, I'm Jonna, but you can call me Jo."

Harper held out her hand. "Harper. You're my new neighbor, yeah? The farrier?"

"I am." I said, shaking her hand, then gestured toward my new place. "I have an blue heeler next door, Shrimp. Promise he's a chill quiet dog. I'd love to introduce you but I'm heading out to a date. You don't know where the Le Casa glamp ground is."

Harper's eye brows raised and a smile similar to that of a snake crawled across her face. "Oh, I know it."

That wasn't ominous.

"Well, I have a date there tonight and I thought it prudent to let another human know, in case it's a plot to murder me."

She crossed her arms and leaned against her doorjamb. "I wouldn't worry about that. But I know where the camp ground is. " She pointed behind me at a gravel path. You follow that gravel path for fifteen minutes' walk, give or take, and you'll find it. There are three raised tents around a huge fire pit. Can't miss it. We use it sometimes when we have family visiting or a "company" cookout. Of course Bart rents them out to campers, but we don't get a lot of them. Not nearly as many as I think he hoped when he invested."

That was too bad. But the rest sounded like a blast. And my parents would absolutely love visiting this place. Knowing I didn't have to keep them on my couch and somewhere on the floor if they decided to visit was a relief.

If nothing else, this date would help put my surroundings into perspective.

Harper rested her head on the doorframe. "Oh, how I do love love."

"You live with a partner?" I asked.

She laughed so hard she snorted. "No. Not at all."

I nodded. "Me neither. I'm trying out that knew app, Miriam's Date-a-Base. Figured, why not? Swipe right enough, I can try an app made by a manic pixie with my taste in marketing materials."

"Hmm." She said, eyebrows knit closer together. "Never heard of it." She shrugged. "I'll have to give it a try."

I put my hands in my pockets and rocked back on my heels. "Well, it was nice to meet you. If I'm not here by morning, whoever I'm meeting on this blind date kidnapped or killed me."

She rolled her eyes and held out her hand. "Phone." I handed it over.

"I'm sure you'll be surprised but perfectly safe. We'll all be at Bingo at the bar, but if you need anything, this is me."

"Thank you, have fun tonight!" I said, as I took a tentative step away and gave her a polite, short wave. "I'll see you tomorrow." and turned to my car as quickly as possible. If I needed to, I could make a quick escape or run them over. Either was good in a weird situation like this.

"Yeah, you will. I want all the juicy details!" Harper shouted after me.

I wasn't sure if I would be giving her any juicy details, but at least I was making friends.

CHAPTER NINE

Starting my car, I cranked the heat. It wasn't snowy, but it was still cold.

The drive took maybe eight minutes for me to go around a hill and through some trees to find the campground. The thick canvas tents hung closed, except for the one in the middle. String lights were lit inside and around the tent, featuring a King size bed, end tables, and even a rug. The lights gave a soft glow in the fading light.

Bart was plating up what he'd cooked from several slow cookers. The wind picked up that second, and I realized the reason the fire wasn't lit and the lights from the tent were on was because of the no-burn ban.

"You just do all the jobs here." I said, wrapping my arms around my middle, looking around for my date to pop out of the shadows.

Bart looked up at me in surprise, then he closed his eyes and nodded as if in silent understanding. "Anything and everything it takes."

"Harper told me you run the camp ground but she didn't tell me you also helped with the meal." I looked around, hoping wherever my date was would be here soon and I wouldn't be blown off again.

There was a small cast-iron tea table big enough for two, sitting just before the tent, so you could see your plate but not be inside.

Bart motioned me to the small table and picked up two plates piled high with pulled pork, a square of cornbread, asparagus, and pork'n beans. He held out my seat for me, and I sat begrudgingly. My date should be doing this, not my boss.

Crossing my legs, I looked around for any signs of car lights. Still nothing.

"Care for a beer?" Bart asked.

I now lived less than fifteen minutes away. I think it was safe to say I'd be able to make it home after a drink or two. "Sure." I said, and watched him open a cooler by the picnic table closer to the fire pit.

He popped open the Mexican beer I'd never had before and set it in front of me. Then he opened one for himself and settled into the seat across from me.

"Oh, I—I didn't realize you were my date." I said, gulping a swig of beer.

Bart took a sip of his own and shrugged. "Is that a problem for you?" He asked.

I mean. I wanted this job. The stability was great, but I wasn't afraid to move around for work. I's been mentally prepared for this whole thing to be a shit show, so what was the worst that could happen? I leave? I was more than capable of moving on if I needed to. Even if that shower was really nice.

And there was something inside me that got giddy at the idea of dating my boss. My hot boss. I wasn't sure if it was the way his shirt hugged him earlier today as he was moving bales of hay, or if it was because it was taboo.

I probably should have cared if the rest of the crew was worried I'd only gotten the job because I was sleeping with the boss, but I had a feeling they knew exactly who he was as a person. And let's be real. No boss had these good of perks for their employees, even if they slept with them.

"I'm willing to see how it plays out." I said.

Bart's smile warmed his face all the way to his eyes. He held his hand over my plate, pointing at the meat. "Pulled pork that's been slow cooking in Kansas City bbq sauce since breakfast. Corn bread casserole, brown sugar beans, and lemon garlic asparagus."

Dinner smelt amazing, and my stomach growled in anticipation.

I took a bite of the pork by itself, and it melted in my mouth. The sauce wasn't too sweet or thick. "What did you add to your sauce?" I asked. Taking another bite, trying to figure out how he'd thinned it down.

Bart held up his beer. "Cerveza."

That would do it. Cut the sweetness just enough, and it would also help tenderize the meat. A man who worked hard, and cooked, was a hot commodity. I could almost let go of my feelings about last night.

"So, what happened last night?" I asked, then stuffed my mouth full of cornbread casserole before I put my foot in there too.

He wiped his mouth with a napkin. "Short answer? I got carried away looking for water."

I wasn't sure what he put in the cornbread casserole, but it tasted much more like a corn cake than a casserole. And I wanted to shove the whole thing down my craw. "What do you mean?"

He signed and rubbed the back of his neck as he leaned back in his chair. "Ranch's well won't make it through the summer. We've had problems with it for years. Had other well's drilled throughout the life of the property, but we live in an arid landscape. Water is a sacristy here. But to keep the Ranch, and all of us going, we need more water."

"And you were just taking a stroll yesterday night looking for water?" I asked. I held my hands out in front of me as if I were holding two sticks. "Did you have those things, the metal sticks that cross to help you find them?"

Bart's eyes squinted at me, and his smile grew even bigger. "Dowsing rods?" He laughed a deep belly laugh as he held his gut. "Something like that."

And he couldn't make time to get to a first date because he was doing woo woo things to find water. I mean, it was a valid fear, and task, but if he was resorting to woo woo methods, maybe this ranch was in worse shape than I thought.

"Were you successful? Finding water?"

He finished his bite of food and shook his head. "No, I'm sorry I missed out on trivia last night. I lost track of time."

I shrugged. "It was your loss. The wings were delicious, and the little old lady group were a hoot to watch play."

"The Gold Diggers, or The Hookers?"

My eyes nearly bulged out of my head. I hadn't been paying attention to the names of the groups, only to the answers to the questions. But they had been wearing matching sweaters. "I'm guessing The Hookers."

Bart wiped his mouth again. "They have a long standing rivalry with The Gold Diggers. Very fun to watch them play."

"I didn't remember seeing any other group of old ladies.

But I'm sure it would have been a hoot to watch them battle it out. The one was funny enough."

Bart's smile fell; his eyebrows drew together. "I'll have to call Phill and check in on Addie. She's the head of The Gold Diggers. Never misses a trivia night. Only happens once a month, and she never misses."

"I hope she's okay."

He nodded his head. "Me too. I'm sure it is if I haven't heard anything. Word moves quick around here."

It was my turn to nod. "I'm sure it does. Which," I licked my lips. "What exactly are we going to tell everyone?" He was right; small towns moved quickly, and I'm sure after talking to Harper, at least the ranch knew we were on a date together.

Bart leaned back into his chair, hands relaxed in his lap. "What do you want to tell them?"

I wanted to scream at him; *I asked first!* But I knew that was childish. If I said I wanted to say we were dating, then it might be me who looked like the gold digger. But if I said, I didn't know, that might look like I wasn't interested. And so far I was very interested! So I shrugged and said, "Depends on how the rest of the date goes."

His smile was back. "I'd like to see how the rest of the night goes as well. I know a little bit about you as an employee but I don't really know you."

"Well, you know I'm a farrier. Before that I worked with my parents in a small traveling circus taking care of the animals. I'm an only child. My parents live in Denver. And until today, I traveled around Colorado, and Wyoming for work. You've met Shrimp. What else is there you'd like to know?"

Bart polished off his cornbread and wiped his mouth.

"You can't say you were in a traveling circus and not elaborate."

"What is there to elaborate on? We moved all the time? I did homework in my parents trailer when I wasn't shoveling shit? It's not as glamourous as it's hyped up to be. The animals were great though."

"But the places you've been. Tell me about your favorite."

"Seattle. Having the beach so close to the mountains and the city is magical."

"Why stay in Colorado?" He asked, taking a swig of his beer.

"My family is here. Sure maybe a few hours drive away but they're close." Family was everything. Yes, I liked my space and freedom, but if they needed me or I needed them; we were there for one another. And having a weekly dinner to look forward to with your parents wasn't a bad thing. "How about you? Where is your favorite place?"

He spread his arms wide. "You're looking at it. Furthest I've been from this ranch is Denver for The Stock Show. Never had a reason to leave."

That was probably the saddest thing he could have told me. I understood travel is a privilege many cannot afford, but from being someone who was lucky enough to see half of the continental United States, that was downright depressing. Even if I had to shovel literal shit the whole way.

"Is there a place you'd like to visit?" I asked and finished off my beans. Not ideal date food, but the man could cook. Who was I to deny either of us these beans?

He polished off his plate, then his beer. "Memphis. I'd like to go see where Elvis lived."

I had not taken him for an Elvis fan. "Is he your favorite musician?"

"No, my Dad's. He was a Vegas "look-alike". It's how he met my mother."

"Ah, so you have performer in your blood too. How did you end up here and not in Vegas?"

Bart crossed his arms. "Mom left my Dad when I was little. And my uncle was the only person he knew who could help raise me. So we moved here and worked the land."

I imagined working a ranch was a lot like working a circus. At least, as a kid growing up in it.

"Did you father ever remarry?"

He shook his head. "Nope. And neither did my uncle."

"So it was just you men? No feminine influence?"

"Mostly."

That mostly sounded loaded. And for a first date, I was not going to dive into that. "Did you always want to work the ranch or was that something thrust upon you by circumstance?" Because I could relate.

"Bit of both." He stood and grabbed two water bottles from the cooler. "I just want to improve one persons life for the better." He set a water bottle in front of me. "The ranch let me do that. I set the rules to make life as equitable as I can make it for others and myself."

He really had. The only way this place could get better was if it were walkable. But like most of Colorado, it sprawled. I guess he'd tried that here with the campground. "You should run for office." I said, finishing off my beer, and cracked open the water.

"Not sure I'm the man for that job." He shrugged. "But, I'm happy to let the professionals know my thoughts." He tipped his water bottle in my direction. "What about you? Always want to be a farrier?"

"No. I wanted to be a Circus Rider like my parents. Specialize in horses. Even trained to ride elephants. But I fell and broke my hip. So, now I still work with and even ride horses but I'll never do acrobatics on the back of one."

"Fuck,, that's scary."

"It wasn't. I was used to falling at that point. Probably should have been more scared. But I felt invincible. Not being able to walk, that was terrifying." I had a doctor tell me I'd never walk again. But thank goodness they'd been wrong. Working full days really took it out of me. Shaving hooves was a physical job under the best of circumstances.

"How about you? Ever break anything?"

"Can't say I have."

"Lucky."

He rubbed his hands along the tops of his legs. "We're both going to be lucky come dessert. Let me clean up and I'll get us my s'mores tiramisu. I'd have loved to have a fire but—"

"Fire restrictions."

"Fire restrictions." He said as he picked up our plates and carried them back to the box I hadn't noticed before, next to the cooler. This man had thought of everything. And he wasn't someone who disregarded a fire ban, thinking it couldn't happen to him.

When he came back, he set down a mason jar with the layered dessert and a spoon. It was so pretty!

"We've got graham cracker crumbs, marshmallow mascarpone, a layer of espresso soaked graham crackers, more marshmallow mascarpone, and chocolate ganache."

I gaped at the detail he had put into all our courses. "Did you go to culinary school?" I asked as I scooped my spoon all the way to the bottom of the jar to get a bit of every layer. The cream was light and marshmallow-sweet. The soaked graham cracker was a little bitter contrast to the chocolate, which was fudge-thick, and the added crunch of the broken graham crackers. It was divine. The perfect bite of s'more, not s'mores. I think my eyes rolled into the back of my head as I groaned in satisfaction.

"Nope." Bart said, then licked his spoon clean. "But my uncle only watched cooking shows. That and golf. Never cared for golf.

We ate a lot of sandwiches between us all, and he always wanted to try new recipes. Even when he didn't know how to cook. Told me every man should know how to feed himself. And that was a goal for him as much as it was for me. We'd experiment in the kitchen. We burned so much food. But we weren't scared to try something new. Or eat our consequences. My dad was happy with his sandwiches, but he ate almost everything we put in front of him. Food's just fun for me." He leaned forward. "And hearing you moan over the taste of my dessert. That's a goal I'll happily commit to. Every. Single. Day."

I licked my lips, and I was pretty sure there wasn't any tiramisu left on them. Yesterday I had been more than happy to let some random person do their best at doing just that. But, now. My boss, this handsome man who could cook like no other, was sitting across from me saying he wanted to make me moan. Every day. And fuck, did I know letting him give it a go was a gamble.

But I never turned down a game of cards. No point in starting now.

CHAPTER
TEN

"You think you're up to the task, every day?"

"I think I can rise to the occasion."

"Mmm." I moaned again around my spoon. I wasn't sure he would be up to the challenge. He did miss our first date in search of water.

"I look forward to seeing you put your money where your mouth is." And I was going to torture myself with wondering what his mouth could do.

Bart chuckled deep in his chest. "Any food allergies?"

Oh, was I totally misreading this? Was he really just talking about food?

"Nope. Never had to worry about it." I said, digging my spoon in for another bite.

He took a bite of his dessert, slowly sucking the spoon clean. "Any preferences? Anything you just cannot stomach?"

I took a deep breath and really thought about it. I liked fresh fruit and veggies. We didn't get a lot of those on the road because, well; it was hard to keep fresh things good for a long time.

"Anything fresh. I'm not really picky." And how could I be? When you come from a life without a fridge. I did love a good pbj with chocolate chips, though. Even after all these years. "I will say, I'm not much for fancy cheese. I've tried charcuterie boards and I can't get past the stink to enjoy the culinary bravado they're supposed to have."

Bart nodded, a sly smile creeping over his face. "Fair."

"How about you? Do you have any allergies?"

He laughed. "No. No allergies for me. And I'm not too fond of stinky cheese either. Brie is the most sophisticated cheese I can stomach." He took a sip of water. "Favorite food?"

Was I going to admit to the man boxed mac n' cheese was my all time favorite food? "I'm not sure I should say."

"So long as it's not squirrel, or fresh pigeon, I think I can handle it."

Thankfully, neither of my parents were the foraging type. We were more of the packaged type. Cans and shelf stable foods were our staple. If we got some barrel juices and toaster pastry's, boy we were doing well that week.

"Boxed mac n cheese." I said, quietly.

"Any particular brand?" He asked, just as softly.

I shook my head. "I like them all." And I did. I even liked the super off brands we'd get visiting the food bank. I think there had been a green mac n' cheese when I was a kid that tasted like they added lime pudding to it, but that was a niche memory I knew no longer existed. Thank goodness.

Bart scraped at the bottom of his mason jar until there was no more dessert, and frankly, so did I.

When we were finished, he took our jars to the box and came back, head bowed. "I'm sorry tonight is such a cloudy night. Even with out the coverage, with all this wind we'd get a lot of flickering and not a whole lot of gazing at the stars."

The wind had blown in a lot of clouds, but it didn't smell like rain or snow. Just gloom. And that was the worst kind of weather. Especially in a drought.

I shrugged. "The company and the delicious food makes up for it."

"I think so too." He leaned over the table as if he'd been punched in the gut. "I guess I best get things packed up. Normally, I'd walk you to your door, but I'm not sure if that's the appropriate move for a first date with your boss."

His features were pinched, like he was about to be sick all over the table.

I wasn't sure that was the appropriate reaction to walking me to my door, but maybe those beans were getting to him. Made me weary about getting sick myself. Maybe it was a good thing he didn't want to start things off by hooking up.

And I was kind of okay with it.

He curled in on himself again. "Are you okay?" I asked.

Bart nodded, eyes cast down at the table. "Yeah." His voice cracked. "I'm fine."

"Can I help you clean up?" I asked, standing up.

He waved at me. "No, no. I've go it. Can you get home on your own?"

I chuckled. "I think I can manage."

Sweat glistened at his brow. "Okay, I'll see you tomorrow. Sweet dreams." He said, raising his face, a smile that was a little bit sad too.

"Sweet dreams." I said, gathered myself, and got into my van.

It wasn't a bad first date.

CHAPTER ELEVEN

I started my van and looked in the side mirror one last time. Bart was now leaning over the picnic table with all the food and started convulsing.

Swinging open the door, I raced back to him. "Bart!" I said, sliding to a stop behind him. "Are you okay?"

His eyes grew big as he looked at me, his body starting to slow and relax. Sweat covered his face, but he slowed his breathing. His eyes narrowed at me, but his shoulders fell.

"I am better, I think."

"What is going on?" I asked, slowly rubbing circles on his back. Did he have a medical condition? Was he allergic to something we ate? Was he on medication he was having a reaction to? That was not normal.

"I cannot say."

I rolled my eyes. "Cool. Have a good night." I said and walked away. I had been with enough guys who couldn't be straight with me, and that was not the road I was going to go down again. We would keep it professional, and this would be the end of it.

I stomped back to the van and slammed the door shut a

little bit harder than necessary. This time I started the car and didn't look back at the campground until just before I went around the bend.

There, in the middle of the campground, was a giant worm. Its mouth, or it's anus, were glowing brightly, as if it were a flashlight. I slammed on the breaks, and gaped at it.

Where was Bart? Was this the craziest form of food poisoning I'd ever had? Had he roofied me? Should I even be driving? Was being able to ask these questions a good indication I was okay, or was I in worse shape than I thought?

I watched the worm as it turned this way, and that, until the glow pointed at me. Then it dug its head down into the dirt and disappeared.

Holding my breath, I waited.

Straining my ears, I listened for any kind of rumble or cracking or anything to prove this was real. That I hadn't completely made this up.

Had I fallen asleep at dinner? That dessert was so rich, maybe I was in a food coma.

Gently, I let off the brake and crawled the rest of the way back to my new home. I didn't feel funny. Maybe a little tired, but I had had longer, much more tiring days.

I could have sworn it was real.

Maybe I was just tired.

The short drive was just like any other drive in the dark. But every shadow and tree had me thinking a giant worm would pop up out of nowhere.

I parked the car, took three steps up to my front door and then I heard it.

A rumble.

Then a crack.

I turned around to the giant worm towering over me

not ten feet away. I fumbled with my keys, whispering, "holly shit, holly shit, holly shit."

Why had I not put them on a different key ring from my other keys? We lived in the boonies. Why had I not left the door unlocked?

The worm didn't make a sound but fell toward me as I struggled to find one of the two new keys.

The worm continued to fall toward me, and I pressed my body flush against the locked door. "Ahhh!" I screamed, closing my eyes and guarding my head with my arms as best I could.

Then, a small thump.

I opened my eyes to see Bart naked and collapsed on my doorstep.

He looked up at me in a daze.

"You have a lot of explaining to do."

CHAPTER TWELVE

My heart was still working on joining me and my slow breaths inside my body.

Bart groaned as he stood up, his height even more pronounced on a shorter step where his eye level was barely at my shoulders. He clenched his jaw and covered himself with his hands."Um, can we take this inside?"

I blinked rapidly and fumbled with the keys. This was not the way I thought I was going to be fumbling for my keys tonight. Sure, I had hoped for a naked man, but this was not the way I had planned things.

Boy, the universe was having a ball with my requests on this one.

I swung the door open. Shrimp raised his head off the couch for a moment, and then rested it back down, not to be bothered but to sleep. As if there hadn't been a giant worm, now man, at my door, whom I was crazy to let into my home. His home? God, this was messy.

Bart closed the door behind himself, then I walked over

to the closet next to the washer and dryer, pulled out my biggest shirt and pair of sweats and threw them at him.

"Here, put these on. " I said and turned before he could catch the clothes and reveal himself.

I thrust my head into the fridge, wishing I had some hard cider or seltzer or something stronger than orange juice. But I didn't, so I poured myself a glass of oj to keep my mouth and hands busy, because I had so many questions.

Bart sat down at the kitchenette, and I leaned against the kitchen sink.

"Go a head, spill it." I said.

Bart looked down at his hands, then back up to me. "I am an augerino. We find water deep within the earth anywhere we claim as our own. This land has been in my family for three generations. And when the water runs dry, we search for every drop of water. I have scoured for months and nothing. No ancient aquifer, or cave system of water lies hidden beneath our feet."

Okay, creepy, but good to know. Colorado had fought over an aquifer not far from here. Hoping there would be one here too wasn't something out of the realm of possibility.

"But since you arrived, I have been almost in a panic following this pull I cannot explain. And I think that pull is you." He ran his fingers through his hair. "At first I thought, it was the excitement of new person. Then when I met you for the first time. This deep feeling, almost longing, but more like a pull, or a sirens song to be near you."

I knew there was no reason for him to be in the barn moving hay bales.

"Being near you feels right." He leaned back into his chair, smiled and rubbed the five o'clock shadow around his mouth. "Before his passing my uncle would reminisce of his Rosa. His Aqua de Vida. I wonder now, if she really was his life's water. The life of this land."

Okay, we had been on a first date and that was swell, but putting this kind of pressure on me was something altogether different. But it didn't stop me from asking, "what happened to Rosa?"

He took a deep sniff, as if holding back a cry. "She died before I got to meet her. My uncle said a piece of him died and the rain has lessened every year since."

I turned to the window; the night sky was still full of clouds, but not the rain kind. "And us being together will bring the rain?"

He crossed his arms, my shirt tugging at the seams so much I wasn't sure my old painting shirt was going to survive. Honestly, it was a sacrifice I could be okay with. The way his shoulders and arms filled the old football-t was worth it.

My mind wanted me to take a few steps back and remember he was once a giant, towering worm, but my body felt fine. I felt as safe now as I did standing on the back of a horse barreling around the center ring. But just because I felt safe didn't mean I was.

"I do not know. He has a life time of hand written journals. Perhaps he has more information there? But, I do know if I leave here tonight the augerino in me will search for water again, and possibly fall upon your stairs once more. I'm not sure either of us want that kind of property damage."

That was probably not a good look for either of us when the neighbors returned. "Do the rest of the ranch workers know you turn into a giant worm?" I asked.

He shook his head. "No. Only you. My father didn't inherit the gene, but he knows of our families curse."

Was it a curse? Or was it a gift? Turning into a giant glowing worm was not glamorous, or sexy, but being able to find water in this environment was an amazing adaptation.

I tipped back the rest of my orange juice and set my cup in the sink. "You can sleep on the couch. Shrimp," I called and patted my leg. "We'll be in the loft."

"No need to make him uncomfortable, I can sleep on the floor."

I rolled my eyes again, ignoring the comment and went upstairs. Shrimp following me closely. "Turn the lights off when you get comfortable." I said at the top of the stairs.

Shrimp settled into the bed, flopping into a ball in the middle of the blankets. I pulled an afghan out from under him and threw it over the banister toward the living room, followed by a spare pillow. "Night. You're making breakfast tomorrow and then we're scouring old journals."

CHAPTER THIRTEEN

I didn't sleep for long. I was too busy thinking the entire night, replaying our evening, looking up augerinos. There was pretty much no information about them available on the internet. Only after I heard Bart's soft snores coming from the couch did I fall asleep. Shrimp curled up against me. I was safe. One time an ex-boyfriend tried to break into the van and Shrimp chased him for two blocks.

Shrimp trotted down the stairs, ready to be let outside, his nails clicking ever so slightly. I would have to pull out the trim board for him after breakfast. Having slept in my clothes because my closet was now in the kitchen, I bounded after him.

Bart lay on the couch, eyes covered with an arm. I stepped out with Shrimp for his morning potty break. The sun had yet to rise, and everyone else who lived here had already left for work.

Shrimp bounded back up the stairs at a run, pushing open the cracked door, jumping onto Bart, still laying on the couch, then up the stairs and back down again. What a way to wake up to the zoomies.

Bart groaned on the couch and sat up. "Good morning."

"Good morning."

He sat there in my clothes, and last night felt like a dream. A very odd dream.

Bart stood, walked over to my fridge, eyed the empty machine, and went to the bathroom. I picked out some clean clothes while I waited for him to exit.

The bathroom door opened, and Bart turned to inspect my equally empty pantry, save the few cans of beans I didn't have anything to go with.

"How did you expect me to make breakfast?" He asked, arms crossed in front of the bathroom doorway.

"I figured being we had to go to your house to read any journals, your stocked kitchen would be sufficient."

He smiled. "If you wanted to see inside my house, all you had to was ask."

I rolled my eyes and squeezed past him. I did want to see inside the large wooden home. Looked like it had a lot of secrets hidden in those walls. "I'm going to take a shower."

"I'll meet you at my place." He said and set off toward my front door.

"You want to walk there in my clothes? What if someone sees you?"

Bart turned around, licked his lips, and asked. "What if they do?"

"I—" My mouth hung open. "What will everyone think? We didn't do anything. And I sure didn't destroy your clothes!" Honestly, if we had done something, I think I would have felt less embarrassed because at least there would have been something worth talking about. "What about turning into a worm?"

He threw his head back with a warm, fully belly laugh. "You did not. But I can see you doing it if I ever gave you reason to. Who cares what they say?" He took a step toward me. "And the only worm controlling me during the day is between my legs. Which I am more than capable of handling."

I'm sure he was.

He took a step toward me and reached his hand up to cup my face. Then kissed both cheeks. "It will be fine." He stepped away and walked out my front door, closing it with a small wave.

I reached up to my face where he'd kissed me, and maybe I was beginning to understand what he meant by a pull. Because I should not have cared as much as I did about a kiss on my cheek.

CHAPTER
FOURTEEN

I'd wanted to make the shower a long one, but knowing the ranch was struggling sure put pep in my process. Shrimp and I loaded up into the van, and we made it back to his house within thirty minutes.

The wooden steps leading up to his house groaned with each step. I rang the doorbell and waited. Shrimp sat like the bestest boy he was at my feet, watching me as we waited for the door to open.

Bart opened the door, still dressed in my shirt and sweats. "Come on in." He said, holding the door open for us.

To the left was a large wooden staircase. On the other side of it looked like a hallway and an open room. Right of the door was a small office fitted with a modern computer and a gaming chair. The house smelt of cigarettes, old wood, and something musky like men's deodorant or cedar. Something manly but nice.

I followed him to the back of the house where a large kitchen led into a large living room fitted with a flat screen and a reclinable couch big enough for an entire basketball team.

He stepped up to the stove and turned the burner back on to the bacon he was cooking in a skillet.

On the table sat four leather bound journals. Each one warn down with time. The pages colored with cigarettes smoke and age.

Bart set down a plate of eggs, bacon, and buttered toast on the table for each of us. "These are my uncles journals. Not a whole lot, but he stopped writing after Rosa died. Maybe there's something in here." He pushed two my way and then pulled the other two closer.

I propped the first book on top of the other and started reading as I dug into my breakfast. The eggs were smooth, not like the rubbery roadside diners we splurged on. And the bread tasted as if he'd made it at home. Probably had.

Page after page, I read about the ranch. How his father had left him an impossible task with no siblings to help. Early entries from his twenties. Some of these things I did not need to know. But the loneliness his uncle had felt, it was so relatable. Being on the road made it hard to find stability. Or gentleness.

We sat there for two hours reading each book. Occasionally I had to stop and ask Bart to translate a Spanish verse. A few times he refused, so I used my phone to look it up. Now I knew how to curse in Spanish.

It was nearly lunchtime when Bart said, "He was so in love with her." He looked up at me, eyes glistening. "*She is the spring my heart has yearned for. The only one who can satisfy my unquenchable thirst for life its self. My Rosa. My Aqua de Vida. I will move mountains if only to see her smile one more day.*"

"When was that?" I asked.

"Shortly after they met." His eyes moved back and forth, reading as quickly as he could. "We're on to something. '*The ranch has never been so green. The rain comes every afternoon, and sometimes even while we sleep. There has never been such a lush summer in the valley.*'"

I picked up our dishes and brought them to the sink. There was no rush in reading the rest of my first book. It was mostly logs of the ranch and how sad he was. A break was well warranted, and I could move my body. Once the dishes were drying on the rack, I opened the back door to let Shrimp out. I watched him do his business and start a sniffing route around the immediate back yard. At least I wasn't the only one who was acting as if this was our own place. I felt like I'd lived here, or at least visited many times over.

It was something I could get used to.

Shrimp ran back into the house and plopped himself down on a rug in front of the large brick fireplace. As if the spot had always been his.

I sat back down and opened the last journal. It was the newest of the bunch; the pages lined and even pretty white still. I fanned them out to see how full it was; when an envelope fell out, addressed to Bartolomé.

"This, is addressed to you." I said, passing Bart the sealed envelope.

He looked up and took it as if it were made of glass. Gently opening the seams on the back to a single page of paper, he read. "*Bartolomé, you were as much my son as your fathers. Maybe more so, as you will no doubt take on my curse. But it is a gift. One I would never trade. Rosa was my best friend. And I would never have met her, if I had not wandered one day to the falls south east of the ranch. She was camping with her family from Denver. And that day we both knew. After we married we made our way back to the falls and made love. It was that day the rains started to fall. I do not know if it was our love, our love making, the falls or being an augerino that brought the rain but I know if you are reading this, you too are searching for water. When my Rosa died a piece of my heart died with her. My Aqua de Vida, was no more and so the water left. Again, I do not know if it was our love or if she was simply magic made human. When you find love. A pull so strong you cannot deny yourself, take them to the falls, or what is left of it. And see if you cannot bring the water back to our land. I am with you, nephew. No mater the choices you make. Love, Uncle."*

"So, you wanna go look at a waterfall?" I asked.

Barts eyes were red from held back tears. "Let me pack a lunch first."

CHAPTER
FIFTEEN

While Bart made lunch, I ran Shrimp in the backyard until he was panting and ready to take a nap. I wanted to bring him everywhere, but if we passed any amount of cattle, he'd start herding them and I just didn't feel like adding that to solving our mystery.

Bart slung the filled cooler over his shoulder with a blanket rolled up under his arm.

I unlocked my van and climbed in. He joined me in the passenger side of the van and pointed me in the direction of the falls. "How long is this drive?" I asked.

"Not long, maybe twenty minute. When I was young we'd play in the creek, but never the spring of the falls. I see why Uncle made a point to visit now. The water is so clear you can see the bottom. Not something you see much around here. It's been years since I've visited. I'm not sure how full it still is."

"Your uncle seems like he was a very good man."

"He was." His voice cracked, and he coughed a couple of times. "I miss him."

I had been lucky not to have lost any of my close family members. The closest loss I could count was when Marty, the ringmaster, passed away. It was the beginning of the end for our circus. No matter how many times we tried to fill the position, it just didn't live up to Marty. And our team of merry performers started finding other places to perform, or like my parents, regular jobs that had a more reliable retirement.

The paved road gave way to a dirt road, not a bit of gravel in sight, so I slowed way down and watched for potholes. Which reminded me. "Those big sink holes Shrimp fell in, they were because of you?"

"Si." he said. "But I don't really remember I've done them. Frustrating when you know they're out there but don't know where until a cow falls inside. The town thinks it's because of all the clay in the soil but really it's me."

"Hmm."

"Hmm?"

He turned to me, and I gave him a glance. "What?"

"You seem very comfortable with the fact I turn into a giant worm."

"I'm intrigued . And I love a good mystery. So, there." It wasn't a solid answer because I felt like I should have run for the hills, but he was still hot and kind. Who was I to judge? "Besides, I lived in a circus for most of my life. Hardly anything can shock me now."

He directed me to park on the side of the road, just out of the way of potential traffic. The snow here had all melted away.

"It's a few minutes hike from the road, but not far." Bart said as he opened the door, grabbed our lunch.

I locked the car and followed him through a path that

curved down the side of a little canyon, where the falls fell into the spring. The steps weren't deep or dangerous.

From here you could see the falls. If these waters weren't what they once looked like, it must have been an intense waterfall. The water cascaded over the edge of the canyon wall we'd just climbed down into a clear pool. You could see where the water once reached. But it was still clean water.

The last step was steep, and Bart held out his hand for me.

There were a good amount of trees here considering the drought we were going through. Bart found one that was to his liking and set up our picnic blanket. We both sat there in silence watching the water, the birds, the sunlight cascade through the branches of the hibernating trees.

"What's for lunch?" I asked. Unsure of what to do now.

"Close your eyes." Bart said, and I did as he asked, listening to the wind move through the trees and the rush of the waterfall not far away.

"Open your mouth." I did as he asked. The bite of apple with peanut butter and a drizzle of hot honey filled my mouth.

It wasn't groan worthy, but it was delicious.

He rustled around in the cooler he'd packed. The sound of glass clinking and a mason jar lid being undone.

"How about this?"

I opened my mouth to a spoonful of that s'mores layered dessert he'd made last night and I did moan again.

"I'm gonna have to keep a few of these jars on hand."

"I won't say no to that."

Our eyes met and his were full of laughter and something more. Something that made low between my legs anticipate so much pleasure. I'd joined the dating app looking for a quick fix, and now I wanted to devour and savor every moment with him.

"Can I kiss you?" he asked.

I leaned forward. Our lips met, and it was as if I were home.

A thunderous crack snapped, and rain began to fall on us, but we would not be stopped by a little water.

EPILOGUE

Bart never insisted I move in with him, but I was at his house more often than my own. Shrimp was more than okay with it. Together we were making ourselves very comfortable at Bart's house.

The crew didn't have any opposition to us being together, like I thought they might. They were mostly just happy to see Bart happy. And in turn, that made me happy.

It had rained for two weeks straight after our visit to the falls. And an hour every day for another two. We visited the falls at least once a week, but we weren't sure if it was the magic of us finding each other or our kiss that made the rain finally fall. But we weren't taking any chances. Sports superstitions had nothing on us.

Sometimes, you just gotta take a risk in life. And boy, was I glad I had.

ABOUT THE AUTHOR

Obsessed with Urban Fantasy since picking up her first Laurell K. Hamilton novel way too young, Brittany has always known she would publish her own someday. What can she say? She likes the burn slow, the spice hot, and everything with a side of mystery and violence.

Brittany lives in Colorado with her all-male family and three cats. When she's not writing, she's hanging on for dear life and doing her best at her second job, Mom.

For more information about Brittany and her books, visit her website at www.brittanylawrence.com. Be sure to sign up for her newsletter to be the first to read deleted scenes, short stories, and exclusive content plus be the first, and sometimes only, to hear about giveaways.

ALSO BY BRITTANY LAWRENCE

Sparks to Ash, A Witches of the Umbre Novel

Kissing A Curse, A Matched by a Unicorn Novella

Coming Soon

Binding Magic, A Witches of the Umbre Novel

Courting Light, A fae high fantasy.

www.ingramcontent.com/pod-product-compliance
Lightning Source LLC
LaVergne TN
LVHW051020080826
845145LV00009B/2715